This book belongs to:

....

....

Retold by Gaby Goldsack
Illustrated by Emma Lake
Language consultant: Betty Root

This edition published by Parragon in 2009

Parragon
Queen Street House
4 Queen Street
Bath BA1 1HE, UK

ISBN 978-1-4075-0657-9

Printed in China

The Enormous Turnip

Bath · New York · Singapore · Hong Kong · Cologne · Delhi · Melbourne

Notes for Parents

These **Gold Stars**® reading books encourage and support children who are learning to read.

Starting to read

• Start by reading the book aloud to your child. Take time to talk about the pictures. They often give clues about the story. The easy-to-read speech bubbles provide an excellent 'joining-in' activity.

• Over time, try to read the same book several times. Gradually, your child will want to read the book aloud with you. It helps to run your finger under the words as you say them.

• Occasionally, stop and encourage your child to continue reading aloud without you. Join in again when your child needs help. This is the next step towards helping your child become an independent reader.

• Finally, your child will be ready to read alone.
Listen carefully and give plenty of praise. Remember to
make reading an enjoyable experience.

Using your stickers
The fun colour stickers in the centre of the book and
fold-out scene board at the back will help your child
re-enact parts of the story, again and again.

Remember these four stages:
• Read the story **to** your child.

• Read the story **with** your child.

• Encourage your child to read **to you.**

• Listen to your child read **alone.**

Once upon a time an old man and an old woman lived in a little cottage. One day, the old man planted some turnip seeds.

Every day, the old man watered the turnip seeds. Soon tiny leaves started to grow.

The old man was pleased. The turnips grew
bigger and bigger. 11

Soon, one turnip was bigger than
the rest.

It kept on growing.

It grew bigger...

...and bigger...

until, one day,
it was enormous!

The old man was very pleased.

One day, the old woman decided to
cook the enormous turnip.

The old man tried to pull it up. He pulled and he pulled. But he could not pull it up. He called to the old woman to help him.

So the old man pulled the turnip,
and the old woman pulled the old man.
They pulled and they pulled.
But they could not pull it up.
The old woman called to
the boy to help.

16

So the old man pulled the turnip,
and the old woman pulled the old man,
and the boy pulled the old woman.

They pulled and they pulled.

But they could not pull it up.

The boy called to the girl to help.

So the old man pulled the turnip,
and the old woman pulled the old man,
and the boy pulled the old woman,
and the girl pulled the boy.

Try again.

They pulled and they pulled.

But they could not pull it up.

Then the girl called to the donkey to help.

So the old man pulled the turnip,
and the old woman pulled the old man,
and the boy pulled the old woman,
and the girl pulled the boy, and the
donkey pulled the girl.

One last try.

They pulled and they pulled.

But they could not pull it up.

The donkey called to the goat to help.

So the old man pulled the turnip,
and the old woman pulled the old man,
and the boy pulled the old woman,
and the girl pulled the boy, and the
donkey pulled the girl, and the
goat pulled the donkey.

Pop!

Oof!

Hee haw!

They pulled and they pulled. Then, pop!
The enormous turnip came flying out of the
ground. Everyone fell down.

It really was the most enormous turnip
they had ever seen. The old woman
cooked the turnip.

Everyone thought the turnip soup was very tasty.

The donkey and goat thought so too.

The old man was very pleased with himself.

Read and Say

How many of these words can you say?
The pictures will help you. Look back
in your book and see if you can
find the words in the story.

soup

goat

woman

girl

donkey

boy

leaves

cottage

man

turnip